*T*horns of love

Don't you feel sorry for these sorrowful eyes,
For this bitter cry, for these cold shivers that I feel,
For my soul that is full of tears?
I would like to remember only those moments
When we ran together through the smoke of life,
But your betrayal finds its place in my thoughts.
If before I could only feel the soft petals of the rose of love,
Now I only feel its thorns piercing me deeply...
If you had a moment of lucidity,
I am convinced that now...
You would have at least a few traces of remorse, of regret,
But you only had the satisfaction that you transformed me
Into a victim... and yes... I admit...
I would like to immerse ourselves together
In the rain of light,
To show you that my grain of love is like a mountain...

S peechless

Can I ever look ahead?
Can I still forget those moments with you?
Can I stop flying through dreams?
Will I be able to have again wings
To escape from this universe full of cruel memories?
Will my heart be able to say goodbye to you?
Where are your blue eyes?
Where are you and why don't you want to come back?
Why can't we both forgive our mistakes?
Why can't I? Why did only I love?
Why did you lie to me like that?
Why did you disappoint me?
I wish I could do something to keep you back
For at least a moment, to touch you and feel you like
mine,
For a kiss and a hug, for everything...
How much did I matter to you?
How many butterflies did you have in your stomach
on our first date?
How emotional were you when you first said "I love
you"?
How much did our break up hurt you,
That bitter taste of loss?
You had to prove to me that you loved me,
That you really wanted to change...
But how could you prove something unreal,
Something that didn't belong to you?
I don't know how to love anymore...
Give me strength to be able to forget you,
Give me strength to be able to love again...

T oday

Today, after a long period of silence,
In which I did not miss you,
In which someone wiped my tears and moistened my lips,
Hugged me tightly to his chest and
Protected me with his love,
I remembered you, I remembered us,
I remembered of my soul that it is still alone,
Although I am not alone…
But I am without you.
In my heart, you still live, you breathe,
I feel you doing good there,
But you don't show up, you shut up.
Maybe I will never understand your attitude,
I will not be able to believe that you did not love me
Even when you were the only one who received my kisses.
I raise my head, look at you, and move on,
Because I am now the nothing you don't need anymore,
The one you once used and then left in a corner...
Forgotten by all.
Why did you do this to my dreams?
Why don't you warm me with your smile,
With your caress?
I miss you so much... I adore you!

Yesterday

Everything seems so close to the present...
The moments were so intense, so sweet,
But still bitter in essence...
Yesterday I should have told you that your absence hurts,
That you hurt me, that I don't feel protected
That I need you,
That I need your comfort.
Yesterday I should have stopped telling you "I love you",
Not forgiving you, not believing in false promises,
Being stronger... or at least not showing you my weakness...
Yesterday I should have started to forget you
And hate you,
I should have ended our relationship and made it all a story,
Wiped away my tears and moved on!
I should have made your heart cry...
Yesterday I should have gotten up,
Even though you crushed me like nothing,
Even though you destroyed me completely,
Even though you didn't care!
Yesterday is today
And everything is repeated once, twice... indefinitely...
Yesterday... I should have done many things,
But I didn't manage to do even a tiny part of them...

S till dreaming

I still dream that I will have you back,
That I will feel your face close to mine again,
That your heartbit will sync with mine,
That your kiss will be gradually sweeter
And that you will stifle me with your tenderness,
That you will be loving
And that the whole world will disappear,
That nothing will matter anymore,
Just me, you and the air that helps us breathe
Just us, my love - just us
Waiting for you here, but waiting it's oppressive,
It's not heavy… it's very heavy.
I hope that one day I will find you by my side,
That you will come back and a rain of stars will fall on us,
That we will giggle again,
That the caresses will find her place among the wounds caused,
That you will change, that pride will be destroyed,
That you will be romantic...
You are my dream without which I can't sleep at night,
You are everything and yet nothing...
You are the man who made me love him,
But also hate him ...
You are the rare flower that withered,
You are the non-existent star in the smoky sky...
I still dream... but I don't know what either...
I don't know if I want you back or I want you away...
I don't know if I have to leave or stay...
I don't know whether to smile or cry...
I don't know whether to love or hate...
And I tend to think that only you can help me solve these riddles, but...
You're gone, I don't see you anymore! I woke up now...

*L*ove

I don't have enough courage to admit that
I can't love a second time,
That I can't feel those butterflies in my stomach on the
first date,
That I can't offer a passionate and sincere kiss,
That I can't hug with the same ardor,
That I can no longer have the same tears of ice,
That I will not be able to get used to it,
That I will no longer be sad
For those few moments when he was not near me
But for those in which I will not see him again.
I don't have the courage
And maybe I don't even want to have...
I don't have the courage to admit that he was to blame,
That I loved too much,
That love hurts and is so malicious,
That it's like an enemy to you,
That it doesn't give you the opportunity to forget,
That it gnaws at you like a worm...
I need support and I don't know where to look for it,
Because all I see around is foreign, expressionless
faces...
And I'm pretending again.
I pretend in order to admit that I need him,
I need him more than ever...
That's all I have the courage to admit and... that I love
him!

Have you forgotten?

Have you forgotten how we met,
How you caressed and touched me,
How was our first date, the first kiss
And the first "I love you"?
You forgot how sweet our reconciliation was,
How much we went through together,
How we managed to solve all the problems,
How close we were when you had no desire
To do something in your life,
How you made declarations of love to me
And I behaved like that a naive child, believing you?
But when did SHE appear?
Did you forget how you changed,
How you took off your mask and hurt me?
Did you forget how you lied to me,
How you couldn't forgive minor mistakes,
And how I forgave major mistakes,
How you treated me with indifference,
How your kisses got cold and I got over it?
Have you forgotten
How I even made the impossible for us to stay together,
To remain US, not just YOU and ME?
Did you forget how we became two strangers
When I still loved you?
Because I didn't... I did not forget.

I *left*

If I left, I did it because I had dignity,
Because indifference and lying
Are things that do not belong in my universe.
Maybe I was to blame,
But it was insignificant for sure...
His mistakes were huge and inexplicable!
I leave you now to take my place,
To help him hurt you too,
To hurt your soul which may now be as pure as mine
once was...
I let you lose confidence in you
And feel how gradually you fall
And you are one step away
From the abyss in which, if you are not cunning
enough, you will fall slowly...
I will wait for you there, you know...
The best thing was that I did not steal his flaws,
That I was not so "strong",
Maybe you will succeed, although I do not want you
to.
I hope you are well and everything is an illusion of
mine...
That I was to blame,
That he was the angel and I was the demon!

Sunset of love

When you hope to forget,
You stop thinking about the consequences...
You just want to get rid of that suffering,
Not realizing that you are causing a much bigger one...
This is how cruel love is,
But at the same time it feeds your dreams,
Without which you couldn't survive in this world
Full of selfishness
That transforms you,
That makes you forget, that makes you stop loving,
That makes you see for yourself
How the last piece of love disappears easily in the fog,
How your lasting love dissolves in the air you breathe,
How it is made of ashes, how it sets…
And you are born again and you love…
But this love also destroys you…
It's like it's the same… it's the same play,
But with other characters…
You didn't even realize when the last love appeared…
Not to mention the disappearance.
You promised that you would not be the same,
That you would change
That you would not even trust yourself,
But you did not succeed…
And you realize that all your life
Youu live the same story
And watch the same sunset of love.

*I*ndifference

Maybe I wouldn't be hurt by your indifference,
Maybe I wouldn't care if you didn't look like him...
Why do you have to remind me of him,
To deepen my wounds?
I would like to believe that I am stunned,
That it is all in my head.
Maybe I miss what used to make me happy,
Maybe I wish I weren't sad anymore!
If I could, I would go far away,
To a place where I would warm my heart
And clear my thoughts.
Only that dry "I love you" still resonates in my mind,
I want to adore you again!
Why did you leave your mark on my heart?
Tonight the stars and the moon will light my way to a
new paradise...
A paradise of tears, 'cause tonight is dark!
I feel so small, so innocuous, so weak,
As if I were inspiring compassion.
Did you bring me so far?
Is this the final outcome or will I recover?
I will definitely miss you,
But I won't look up for you anymore... I promise!

I' d wish

I'd wish I could tell you how I feel,
I'd wish I can tell you that I still love you
And I miss you so much.
I'd wish my wounds wouldn't hurt so much,
That I could get over these moments
And that my smile could be real.
I'd wish I could get closer to your face,
Destroy the distance between us,
Sprinkle petals of red roses
(You know how much I like them)
Over our lives, over us.
I would like you to give up the pride
And you to be like you used to be.
I would like to believe that time stood still
And it did not run out,
So I would not be so astonished
Of how long I was able to love you
Without receiving anything in return.
I would like to believe your lies again and again,
Even at the risk of rediscovering them,
At the risk of suffering once more,
Of dedicating my tears to you.
I'd wish I could shake your hand,
See your eyes twinkle again,
So that the gray would take on color,
So that my heart would no longer hurt,
So that I could no longer feel your absence,
So that I could feel your warmth,
So that we could smile and joke together again,
Get rid of the monotony that might come between us,
Be your talisman.
I would like you to love me and be yours again!
Give me back my dreams and hopes!

W*aiting*

The enigma of perfect love is waiting.
What is the point of
Always being with the wrong person
And then suffering from hypocrisy,
Despite your awareness that everything is unfair?
For gaining an experience?
Is there anyone who prefers suffering
Just to have a helpless experience?
Wouldn't you choose childishness
And hope that you will have the full experience when
finding the perfect love?
Waiting is the "key to success"
And your patience will be rewarded...
But if you don't wait for the perfect love you try to
find it,
Knowing you won't find it,
Can you still hope to have it?
Do you think your mistake will be rewarded
And not punished?
Do you think time is reversible?
Wait for an answer... don't look for it...
Because you might lose it too,
You might lose everything. Wait!

I am looking for

I am looking for a smile without tears,
I am looking for a love without traces of pride,
I am looking for an honest answer,
Pure feelings, an "I love you"
Said from the bottom of my soul
And a person who deserves sacrifice.
I'm looking for smoke where everything is ashes,
I'm looking for hopes where everything is long gone.
I'm looking for love when there's only hatred around...
I'm looking for a drop in the rain...
I'm looking for the moon when there's only sun in the sky,
I'm looking for stars in dark nights,
I'm looking for light in the dark,
A wish that I want, sincerity in a look and a kiss.
I'm looking for a reason to say "yes",
A second in the thousands of minutes,
A memory in tears and a tear in feelings,
Old feelings, forgotten and abandoned,
Feelings that I would like to slip through the dust of a life.
I'm looking for a a dream I can rely on,
An innocent smile, a trace of childishness.
I'm looking... but I can't find anything!

Coincidences

How do I fight when I get so many hopes?
From whom do I receive them?
From you or from destiny?
But... how can you give them to me,
When you don't even look at me,
When you don't even know me,
When a whole life separates us,
When that dry "Hey" doesn't even exist anymore,
But it was...
Is it fiction or destiny makes me stop fighting against you,
Against everything that seems to unite us,
Against the dream that convinced me
That I will soon forget you?
What's going on?
I'd rather wish everything be against a possible reconciliation,
Because otherwise the tears will come again...
How painful it is to be by your side
And not be able to touch you,
To be in front of you and not be able to kiss you,
For me to exist and you not caring...
It's painful to love and hate you,
To keep your memory and to look at you,
Not being able to hold you back
Not wanting you anymore...
How to fight if no one helps me,
If everything destroys me and I am left with nothing,
If I no longer have ambition?
I can't... that's enough for me!

# Why?

Why did you change if you taught me to love?
To teach me to resent you with the same intensity?
Why can't you forgive?
To not be able to relive all those euphoric moments?
Why can't we be tied to the same thread of life?
Why do we hide behind appearances?
Why can't we tell ourselves the truth
And we do nothing but build a wall
That gradually grows stronger and destroys our hopes?
Why can't you acknowledge how you really feel?
I support myself on some dreams ...

Color

Today I learned that you paint your life
The way you want,
That a simple stain of color
Can make as much sense as it can ruin everything...
I ruined everything,
I chose to forgive and not to change,
Not to forget and to live the moment, n
Nt to take revenge and to continue to love.
I chose to suffer and freeze in the cold of life,
To fall without getting up, but still...
I'm up now ... and you know what?
Nobody helped me,
Because everyone is lazy and self-centered.
No matter what I or you or others do,
I promise to stand up...
Just to prove to you that I've always been above you,
That I've always been one step ahead of you,
And I've been the only one who guided you,
That my painting is warmer than yours,
That it is more vivid and the color is more intense,
That no matter what happens,
I will not change and my life will be full of color!

If I were

If I were a swallow,
I would take you with me to the heights of heaven,
Where everything takes on color and love can be revived.
If I were a mermaid,
I would carry you through the foaming waves of the sea.
You would watch the sunset and sunrise
With someone who loves you.
If I were an angel,
I would watch over you at all times.
I'd be by your side 61 seconds out of 60.
I'd be there without you knowing.
If I were a fairy like you used to treat me,
I would fulfill all your desires and wrap you
In a mysterious spell.
But it's just me... and I...
I'd like to know
Why you made me believe that our souls came together
And we lived as one person,
But above all I'd like to know if you loved.
I suffer now.
You have caused me wounds that have not yet disappeared
And it presses me, making me not being myself.
I would like you to reappear as a ray in my life.
I can't be anything without you,
It's just me.
I don't like that you can't see how much I love you,
How much I miss you...
And everything could be so simple.
All you have to do is reach out... and I... I'd be there!

Only you

Are you here?
I see you and I can't believe I found you...
Your lascivious gaze,
Your jerky breath,
They all make me feel like I'm in a dream with you...
I feel my heart flood in this exorbitant euphoria
And just looking at you for a moment...
I know that our feelings are similar and so intense.
I close my eyelids for a moment
And I feel you in every pore,
I want to see you again,
I want to tremble with emotion and get lost in your
eyes... I want you to make me smile when I'm upset,
To soothe my pain with simple words,
To stop the tumult in my heart and become myself
again...!

D*oes it hurt?*

Does infinite but unshared love hurt?
Indifference and truth?
Does it hurt when your loved one lies to you?
But when you cheat
And fall into the abyss
Or when your wings start to break in flight
And you collapse and no one helps you?
Does it hurt when your words start to dry up
Because of him, because of the deep disappointment,
Or when you live a dream
Even though you woke up a long time ago,
When you hope and receive nothing?
Does it hurt that you found out the truth too late,
That your wounds seem to last forever,
That he doesn't even look at you as someone he knows?
Is it that your poems are written in tears,
Tears that are deeply ingrained in your face,
That you have matured too much
As a result of this suffering, this experience,
And that you have lost all confidence, childishness?
Does it hurt because it's too late to say how you feel,
To say something or to hope?
But why should it hurt you?
Why not hurt him?
What did you lose?
Nothing... then what changed you or why?

Desire and power

In time, you realize the significance
Of things that were previously imperceptible.
In time, you realize that desire
Is not enough to achieve a dream…
A dream that usually can easily become something real,
But in those moments it can be likened to
Escaping from your own world,
To perfect love.
Forgetting… what is it?
Making a dream come true? I think so...
You want to forget, but you can't...
The power you have is negligible,
But it gradually increases
With the wounds you are inflicted!
At least they're helpful on the one hand,
Because it's enough to hurt when they start bleeding…
But it's not enough!
You tend to think that time is your enemy,
That it multiplies your wounds.
Actually... is anyone close to you?
Is time the only enemy?
What is the difference between desire and power?
Is power the enemy of desire?
If it wouldn't existed,
It would have been possible
For you to be mine again.
Or would have been possible to forget you?
I don't know what I would have chosen...
Anyway you hurt me whether you are or not mine.
My wish no longer exists!
I let it all go... I love you anyway!

Decision

Maybe it will be hard for me or maybe I will recover,
I will cry or I will smile,
I will stay or I will leave.
I won't find out until after a long time,
During which, I hope I don't miss you anymore.
I don't know if it will be good or not,
But for now I think it's the best decision...
I'll leave, I won't suffocate you with my love,
I'll leave you with her!
It's too late and yet it's too early...
Now I just want to let you know
That the little problem is starting to go away,
That time is starting to become supportive,
That time is startin not to give me back your cruel memory.
I hope, as always, that this is the last letter...
All I'm asking for is that you show up once more,
Even at a distance, even for a second, even with her...

*P*ain

The disappointment of love
Is the greatest and with it come the others…
Because a disappointment precedes a series of sufferings.
Everything seems so cruel, so hard to bear…
An insignificant blow becomes a difficulty,
A sadness becomes a game of tears,
A love becomes... hate?
Can you lie so much?
Can you say you hate
When you actually love more than ever?
Love does not change, it is invincible... but why?
You want everything to stay the same,
And for her to change.
But it's actually the opposite.
Why do you lie to yourself,
That you prefer him to be happy
Even if it's not you, even in her arms?
Why lie that you could forgive
And that your love would be eternal?
Be honest!
Acknowledge that this love
Will remain just a memory and pain...
Not a dream, not a hope, not perfection!
But is there anything left of that love?
Didn't he destroy it?
Didn't you destroy it together?
Isn't it routine now?
You may have forgotten him...
But you keep that moment of happiness
As something sacred
And that makes you continue to "love",
It makes you continue to remember
With enthusiasm a love that was "perfect".

Without you

There can be smiles without joy,
Tears without pain,
Sky without sun,
Night without stars,
but I can't exist without you.
I can reach the intangible, you know?
I love even though I would like to hate...
But only with you...
Around you, the old self disappears,
That old self that will soon die because of you.
I'm better now,
Because I know how to forgive,
I know how to forget,
I know how to enjoy life like a butterfly,
I know one disappointment does not precede another,
I know the smile will always be sweeter after a tear,
That everything seems easier
When you are close to me, when you protect me...
Maybe sometimes you are
A more important person than me,
Maybe I would like you to be well,
Even though I'm not...
And you certainly deserve it, because you...
You are... my friend!

A byss of suffering

I don't think you're sorry,
I don't think love can change you,
But is it love what you feel
Or you are overwhelmed by your pride?
Your selfish, immeasurable pride?
Yes... that is...
Although I would love you to suffer,
To feel betrayed,
To be invaded by guilt,
Because then it mattered more what others said.
You were too childish to realize that betrayal pays off.
I warned you this will be the case,
That the hourglass sand will flow in my favor
And you passively told me:
"You can't do anything about it."
And you were right. I didn't do anything.
It all came naturally... but it's too late for you now,
It's too late to relive those moments...
Now memory is the only thing that feeds you.
I was so waiting for this moment,
The moment when I am the one who drags you into the abyss of suffering!

I '*m crying*

I'm crying… Just like a cut ficus,
Trying to cling to the side that stays in the pot,
That stays alive!
That's how I felt when we broke up…
I close my eyes and I wish
I could see the enchantment of winter,
The excitement of the holidays,
But among the bare trees,
Among the twilight lights in people's houses,
Among a few breezes of the wind,
Among the twinkling stars and among the snowflakes,
I see only melancholy, desolation, and bitterness.
I wish I could say that life goes on,
That I will always have what I wanted,
That I didn't even need you,
That I drove you away and you didn't leave...
I open my eyes
And I see myself in front of a stained mirror,
With tears in my eyes, with a flushed face,
I see that childish little girl
Who doesn't feel able to forget
And always clings to the past,
To her lost moments,
A little girl who would give oxygen
In exchange for eternal love!
Tell me, you, who are "expert" in change:
How can I mobilize myself,
How can I dictate to the subconscious to be passive,
To choose a path on which
There are only butterflies and roses,
Only light and pure love,
And not sadness and imperfection...?
If I'd found her,
Would you go with me and leave everything for us?

*L*ove

Why does everything that is beautiful ends in a second,
And what you dislike tends to last indefinitely?
Why does the first love grind your heart with every pulse?
And why does everyone become a poet
When they reache love, as Plato said?
I think that relativity in this world
Has only one exception and that is suffering...
Love is a game like any other,
From which only one emerges victorious
And the one who loses feels nothing!
Is it fair what is happening?
Is it fair that all your sacrifices prove to be in vain?
Why when you love you catch wings
And try to fly,
Even though you know you will never succeed?
Why forgive when you shouldn't?
Why do you love when you should hate?
Why is everything so complicated,
When it could be so easy?
In fact... is there love
Or do we all dream of reaching the unreal?
And here I am referring to a simple love,
Not a perfect one.
I think these will always be questions
That no one will be able to answer!

*T*ear

It is said that a smile,
When you are sad,
Is more painful than a tear…
No… nothing is more painful than a tear,
That tear that may not even exist,
Because all were wasted by a broken heart…
When they start to flow they tend not to stop,
They tend to destroy you more…
And you stop… and ask yourself:
"Why am I crying?",
But you keep crying without your approval.
You are convinced that
A tear can't bring the past back to life,
Like a star can't make night...
A tear and that's it...
She's the only one who kills you... or not?
Isn't it a good memory
Will bring you joy as
You were able to live the moment?
Doesn't one look from him
Delight you as you both live under the same sky?
Doesn't a received hope
Make you feel euphoric and dreamy?
All of this gives you at least a smile, a relief...
You see?
Only the tear hurts, that drop on your face...
And yet it is what keeps the love intact...
If it weren't for the tear,
Wouldn't boredom, monotony, intervene?
A tear does everything ...

Is it worth it?

The eternal question: is it worth it?
Is it worth it to suffer
And want to keep at least a memory with him?
The eternal answer... I don't know...
But how long will this take?
How long will it take for you
To realize that it's NOT worth it,
That it's useless to keep him in your mind
When he didn't care about you
From the first moment?
Sometimes you think rationally
And you are willing to leave everything in the past,
To learn from your mistakes... but other times?
Where is that side of you that thinks positively?
Why does the skeptical side reappear?
As in any similar situation,
There is a struggle between optimism and pessimism...
Why would pessimism win?
Why are you destroying yourself?
Why choose suffering,
When happiness is so close to you?
Why did you change so much
For a love that didn't even exist...
Because love involves two people...
You can't love for both of you.
Like you also cannot fight
For a love that has always been imperfect!
Don't you think that the time of pessimism is over,
That so many painful moments
Have been enough?
That there is now room for a new beginning,
That does not include him,
That the eternal answer "I don't know"

Should become an imposing NO?
Don't you think it's over,
Even though you still haven't figured it out?
Does it still worth it?

G ratitude

What a dream I live
With the person who taught me to love again,
Who was by my side,
Even if I went through hard times,
Even if I could only cry,
Drown myself in tears,
Even if at first I felt that
I could not know again the feeling of love,
The feeling that changes you,
That makes you believe that perfection exists
And is made up of you and the one next to you,
By your side...
Thank you for knowing
How to appreciate my weaknesses,
That you knew myy heart was not completely
destroyed,
That a corner of it was untouched, it was pure...
That you knew how to show me
Everything can be forgotten,
If you have the will and help...
I love you,
Because you gave me the strength to go on,
Because you were the only one
Who told me every moment how special I am,
The only one who told me not to give up a love,
I admire you,
Because you are the only one who exists for me,
Because my heart is yours
And you always knew
How to take care of it... I love you!

*S*tory

... I'm here, you're there ...
I'm taking a step and that's enough,
Because I'm next to you...
Maybe that's how I've always been,
Just a step away!
And it's a new love,
A new smile,
A new beginning!
Together we built a crystal globe,
In which our love gradually settled.
I thought this is how we would protect it,
But no...
We were both too childish,
Or maybe just you,
Or maybe just me...
The globe broke and love became more sensitive,
Far too sensitive for you...
Love remained only for me, being bigger.
You walked away...
But was it only one step between us?
If I managed to get back to you,
Would everything have been resumes?
I tend to think so,
I tend to think that step
Would have led me back into the abyss,
By no means into the arms of love.
I tend to think that you didn't even exist
Or that you left before you came...
A new love, a new smile, a new beginning...
Maybe all of that existed,
But that beginning preceded such an end,
Preceded these lines
Written by the one who once loved you...
Preceded a new story!

We in the past... just myself now!

Why did you have to leave
And leave me here alone without you?
Will you be back?
It will be too late.
Someone else knew how to make me smile,
To see light in the dark,
To notice the purity of a snowdrop,
When it was a simple flower,
To feel the intoxicating scent of the iris
When it displeased me...
It's risky to love again,
To trust in love, affection and tenderness,
After the tumult in my heart...
I wish I could love him,
He deserves everything...
But you don't let me go...
Like always, you are to blame for everything.
Why did you have to be so self-centered?
Why?
Despite everything that has happened,
The deep disappointment you have caused me,
I still love you and I will always do,
Although you could never be a part of my life again!

I don't know

I don't know how long I will last,
How many tears I am still holding
Or when I will smile again.
I don't know if I should get closer or further away,
If I should stay or turn into a shadow,
If I still have to offer love,
When I only receive hatred,
If there's any point in hoping,
When everyone destroys my dreams.
I don't know if I should continue or stop,
If I can find you in the same place,
Where I left you,
If my hands still feel you,
If your scent persists in my body,
If you've ever been close to me.
I still can't get used to the fact
We areno longer together...
Come back, honey!
I'll be waiting for you forever!
Your words have remained imprinted in my memory
And I always hope I will hear them again someday...
All I have left are the memories of our days,
The days when my smile made sense,
When my breath felt yours!

Change

Stop!
My tears have soaked my wounds too much.
I thought time would heal them faster,
But in fact it infects them...
They've deepened,
They've become too deep to bear...
I don't know when I'll forget you.
I don't even know if it's love or hate
That I feel for you,
If it's a tear or a smile on my face,
If it's you or me.
I know I'm a little skeptical often,
But that feeds me, that makes me live...
If I thought I could forget you tomorrow,
That I'd be able to put everything that was between us
in a box
And then I'd throw it in the sea,
That I could give up dreaming you are still by my
side,
That I could remove the tear with a smile,
That I might not love you anymore,
Then I would surely forget what love is...
So it's best to be skeptical as much as possible.
I think it's better for me
To be addicted to anything that has to do with you,
It's better for me not to forget you,
Even though it means suffering...
How much you've changed me!

I don't miss you

How good it is
When you can look back
And realize that there is
Not a shred of that love left,
That you don't miss him that much,
That you can be yourself,
Despite the fact that you have suffered someday,
That you can stop crying,
That the empty place next to you
Doesn't hurt anymore,
That a tear now means happiness, fulfillment,
That not everything seems black and obscure anymore,
That everything has become a simple memory,
A memory that doesn't kill you anymore...
Now everything has taken on color,
Everything has revived!
I'd wish this change had come sooner...
A new world, new people...
Everything is so different, but it's the same...
Now I don't miss you anymore,
You can't hurt me anymore,
You can't give me vain hopes anymore...
I'm not the old me anymore...
It's magical, but also tragic, because...
Everything is a lie!

R *eally?*

It's weird how one person
Can change your life,
How he can teach you certain things
You'd rather not know —
And why do you think of HIM
Every time you listen to a love song?
Why do you see only HIM in every man?
Why do you dream of being alone with HIM?
Why doesn't his memory give you peace
And make you not trust your own strength?
Why do you become euphoric
When you think about the moments
You spent with him,
But melancholy when you think about
The disappointments he caused you?
Why do you dream of an impossible reconciliation?
Why don't you want to forget him?
Why do you feel the same way
When you first looked at him?
Why does that non-existent "hey" hurt so much?
Why do you want to fall asleep
Just to have him in your dreams?
Why do you regret not forgiving now?...
Because you love HIM?

*L*ooking back

Looking back and what do I see?
Only regrets and unpleasant memories,
Only pleasant moments and hopes...
And I wonder why?
Why do I think only of the moments
When I was happy even though they were few?
Why does it hurt so much
That I'm not close to you?
I see you every day
And in every look of yours I find a hope...
And yet hope that probably
Only exists in my imagination.
My thoughts fly to the past,
To the moments with you
And I want to fly into the future,
To forget everything, you, me, us...
It would have been better
You not to appear in my life,
For me to still be the innocent little human
Who didn't know how to love.
I wish I hadn't met you
Or fallen into your trap...
And yet your words were
So plausible, same as the feelings.
My conscience tells me to stop,
But my heart? She fails...
The intrinsic loves
With the greatest intensity
And it burns me, it melts me... it's so hard...

K idnap my heart!

... and yes! I feel like
I'm missing something,
Maybe that stolen kiss,
Maybe that jerky breath,
Your face looking for me,
Your eyes waiting for my gaze,
Your hand touching mine,
Your tender hug and why not,
Just everything, just you?
I don't want to fool anyone
By saying that it was love at first sight...
But at first touch!
And I like that we are
Two innocent human beings
Who don't know what they want,
We don't know how to express ourselves,
But we still tremble with emotion
When we meet,
When we feel each other
And die of the desire to be close to each other,
To remove the shyness...
Once again, life proves to me
That sometimes love is right next to you,
But it comes at the right time,
When hope needs one more moment
To sink into nothingness.
Let the thoughts fly and the dreams come true!
And I'm just telling you: kidnap my heart!

*F*eelings

Sometimes I want to forget about you,
But other times I want to keep
All our moments in one memory…
Or rather the moments spent with you,
Because those are no longer ours
Because of you…
You didn't want to fight the others,
But especially against your pride.
I'm sorry that everything fell apart so easily,
I'm sorry that I loved
When I should have been passive,
When I shouldn't have opened my heart.
I regret that even now
I cannot treat you with indifference,
After so many days that have passed,
Only because they had to pass,
Days when I cried and was locked in myself,
Days when only you
Could have relieved my pain,
Days in which I waited for you
And you did not come,
Because it was all about HER, YOU,
It was all about both og YOU.
How I wish you hadn't lost myself,
You hadn't lied so much,
You hadn't played with me,
Taking advantage of my innocence.
I regret that even now my face is wet with tears,
That I always keep writing to you,
Even though you don't deserve it...
In fact I regret that I have feelings for you,
Whether they are hate or love,
Or they are both at the same time.
I'm sorry you were by my side once!

*A*nd yet I hope

It's too late…
It's been too long since then,
To be able to accurately remember
Everything that happened between us...
However now I see you
Among my thoughts and memories...
You were the first...
The first flight to the unreal,
The eternal dream and, at the same time,
My help towards maturity,
Towards the liberation from childhood,
But... can't I forget that?
Is that why a part of me is always by your side?
... maybe now I'm more childish than ever,
Thinking that everything
Can be forgotten so easily...
I wish you could truly love soon
And to have at least a piece of my suffering.
I would like you to love me...
And yet I hope to forget you...
And yet I hope you do not forget me!

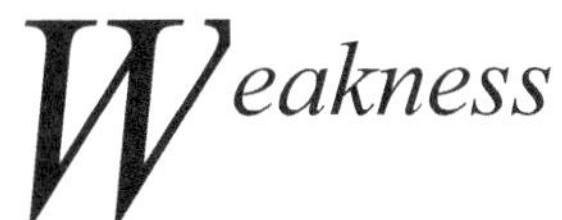eakness

You know that I am weak,
That my lips are still waiting for you,
That my shoulder will always support you,
That I will believe you
When you tell me you miss me,
That I will believe you
When you tell me you were wrong
And that you want me back.
You know I can't say no.
The moments when I didn't see you
Made me stronger,
Made me forget about you for a few seconds,
Throw the bag of memories in the rain,
For them to get wet... to dissipate...
They made my thirst for you to crumble...
But for what?
It was useless anyway...
The sight of your eyes
Turned me into the same person
A person with so many weaknesses,
Who is dependent on you...
Who would give anything
Just for a moment when you possesses her,
When her burned lips are healed by you,
In which her broken heart
Begins to throb again with force,
A moment in which no matter what happens
She cannot rise...

My star... your star

...Yes!
I know it was hard for you,
A twilight light appeared... a star...
Your falling star and with it...
Your self-centered desire to own me, to...
Be together!
You seemed so detached from reality,
From any interaction with anyone else,
Except for myself.
But the star rose, it resumed its place in the sky,
Among the thicket of the cosmos,
Knowing that your desire
Was not strong enough to be fulfilled,
It was not plausible enough for a... star!
And yet the dream came true...
Those beautiful moments were so ephemeral...
My memories hurt and...
Your star became my star.
It came down from there...
Into the attic and it stayed,
Because my desire was of the highest intensity,
I wanted to look at you,
To hate you
And the star believed me;
It knew it was best for you, for me, for us...
And your star... it's mine now!

1 hate you

I hate you because
I can't be happy because of you,
Because my smile looks like a tear,
Love - hate,
Light - darkness...
Why can't you leave for good?
You don't care anyway,
You don't feel my pain...
Why do you make me bleed inside,
Cry when everyone laughs,
Hate when everyone loves?
When this whole story
Seemed to run away,
You came back,
You as a memory,
You as an illusion,
You as a plausible dream...
And again everything fell apart...
I begin to get used to the suffering,
To adore this feeling called hatred,
To see only darkness, not to be myself ...
And I think I like it!
I'm starting to be like you,
An impassive person,
A person who can't see beyond appearances,
An egocentric person,
A person who lives only to pollute souls,
To destroy everything that's been built...
A person who doesn't deserve to live ,
A person who will gradually die
And be born again,
To realize that he was wrong too much
And now it is too late to fix something,
It is too late to apologize,

It is too late to live again...
And he prefers to die, but not be born again.
Look... that's how I am now...
I don't hate you anymore...
Or maybe I hate you
Just because you taught me
To love and I didn't want to know that,
I just wanted to hate… to hate you!

*B*etrayal

It hurts so much
The poison arrow stuck
In the heart of a loved one…
The disappointment is so big,
The full trust of so long is shattered
In a single moment, in the moment of truth.
Who else can you trust
Where there is only envy and hatred around,
When apparently it was
Just appreciation and love…?
How ironic is life,
How ironic is the probable!
Accepting the real is so difficult
In the moments of balance,
In the moments when the masks are destroyed.
You have only one hope left,
Which you hope will not be powdered too...
Hope that belongs to the other "truth",
That really seems to be true...
Where you find solace and understanding,
Love and self-confidence,
At least in yourself...
Disappointment has reached the brink of ruin!
You have managed to destroy it
And once again
You prove that you are strong,
You prove that there is no more skepticism in your way.
Everything is as it should always be!

You will be

False promises and vain hopes…
That's all I received from you…
It wasn't love, tenderness or affection,
As I would have preferred.
Was it luck or bad luck
That I ever had you by my side?
"I will be" was the only thing you said...
But when did you want to be
Or rather when you wanted to change
For a person you were just supposed to love
And take care of her heart,
That you were by her side no matter what
That you gave her sincerity?
How well you could hide,
Look like something you weren't,
Look like I wanted you to be.
How much your eyes lied
That seemed to look at me so gentle and loving.
How much you lied to me that I am your life... "I will be" ...
You will be the same as before,
You will not change, but I will...
I will no longer be myself,
I will no longer be the one
Who knew how to forgive and to love,
Who knew when to leave and when to come,
Who cares about everyone.
I will be as I always should have been:
Impassive and self-centered.
Now I don't care if you're still there or not.
You can stay where you are,
Because I don't care anymore!
You will be... but alone!

*E*nough

Everything was ephemeral…
I knew how to appreciate you,
To forgive you,
To love you,
To be by your side,
To be your friend, not only my girlfriend,
To help you.
Then I found out what hate is,
How you really were,
I found out that I didn't know you well enough,
That hate and love are the same flower,
The only difference being that...
Love has thorns... yes!
Why for a moment of excitement
Do you have to offer so much more in return?
Why is what you do not appreciated?
Why is good rewarded with evil?
Why am I looking for smoke
Where everything is ash?
Why am I looking for hope
Where everything is long gone?
Why are feelings rare flowers?
I loved you, but it wasn't enough...

One-night dream

What an angelic face and what a frail body,
Like deities… you know?
I so desperately want to be close to you,
To feel the warmth of your body,
To look into your eyes to the end of eternity,
To apologize that
I loved you maybe too much and...
To destroy my dream,
To turn it into a nightmare,
How I should have probably perceived it from the
beginning,
I should have considered you dull
And pierce your heart
With the most atrocious feeling for yourself,
So that you consider yourself so innocuous,
To be demoralized.
My one-night dream metamorphosed
Into a grand aspiration.
Don't wait for me
To find your tracks and hug you,
Because I won't... I'll leave
And I leave here
All my feelings of pure love for you...
I'm already gone, I don't idealize you anymore!

Appearances

No... I can't help but get caught up
in appearances,
when there are so many things
that force me to hide.
There are so many circumstances
in which I have to look happy, strong,
so I cannot get any closer to the abyss.
The more pharisaical I am,
the farther I go from failure.

This is not the life I wanted.
I am spinning
In a continuous whirlwind of dirty deeds,
of spoken words, but which
would have been much wise
to keep them in my soul,
to close them in a corner of it
and to put the lock
that cannot be untied, broken...
but I can often throw words, deeds, feelings
into this corner...
So I can feel better,
I can free myself from anger and contempt
for some moments in my life.

I never thought I could say such words,
that I would be so self-centered and say:
"I want to be happy and,
if it involves the happiness of others,
I will not oppose it.
I don't care about the other.
Let them create
their own globe of happiness! if they can… "

There are so many dusty threads here,
threads that I gradually and slowly swallow.
They will destroy me, I know!
Exorbitant ambition and skepticism
will destroy me too!
I will go through a stage where
weakness will gradually settle in my body,
preparing for the great victory.
It will dominate me.

I am just someone who
sometimes does not know what to say,
someone underestimated by many,
appreciated by few and
understood by no one,
because no one will ever know
everything that is in my soul,
because I am also afraid to discover another me,
other feelings,
another character,
another face…
What if she will suffer more than I do?
I prefer not to risk…
anyway, I will not lose anything.
When fear moves to another body,
I will take risks,
because at that moment,
I will be sure that I will win!
Now I have too many doubts.

*T*oday

We all know that
sometimes we need more,
that what we receive is
insignificant compared to what we offer.
Life no longer gives us the opportunity
to ask for our rights,
to dream and to say:
"I want more. I need something better"
There are times when all we want is
to take it from the beginning,
to fix our mistakes, right?
We all say that,
we all want the impossible and yet
we have a glimmer of hope there.
But without knowing who feeds it,
who helps it mature.
When we wait for everything to be fine,
we receive a new disappointment,
a new tear.
Yes, that's right!
I'm telling the truth!
Why being optimistic,
why letting skepticism aside,
why seeing the good side of things
when it moved away
from the moment I was first disappointed?
There is nothing good left!
Maybe I gave up on him,
maybe I was the one who left him...
or maybe I didn't deserve to be with him.
When I had the opportunity to choose,
I wasn't careful enough, and now that,
I guess,
I have something better,

I can't enjoy him,
I feel that I can no longer love or
maybe I am wrong.
I was so evil that now I have to pay,
through suffering,
through regrets,
through these bitter tears!
I took advantage of others,
of the pure feelings of
those who actually deified me.
In fact, I don't know... all I do is guess!

Bliss

Again that constant state of enchantment,
again the same sweet caresses,
the same kisses full of passion.
In fact, they are not the same,
because they were essentially bitter,
those feelings were only seemingly tender.
These are plausible instead,
palpable and so magnificent.
Eden appears and invites you inside,
it offers you that fascination,
that something you needed for a long time,
without which you could have not
lived too long,
which you missed.

The weakness you possessed,
not long ago,
it disappeared without a trace,
without marking you,
without leaving its mark
on a part of your body… and you are happy!
Now, even insignificant things
seem to bring you splashes,
which will form a universe,
from an incomparable euphoria.
Tears, regrets or nights full of insomnia,
all have disappeared now.
You see how much you have to endure
to receive what you want,
how much hope you have in your soul
only for a few moments of euphoria,
which you hope will last indefinitely
or like time to stop in place for you,
to feel their essence,

to fully enjoy them,
not to lose them again.

You are so happy now,
when all evil seems to have fallen
into nothingness forever…
and you keep hoping,
you must always know
how to hope.
Hope, even if life
is not a good friend at all times
and it turns into a fierce enemy,
even if everything seems to be against you
and any loved one is gone
and bliss disappears,
because that way
you will always be one step ahead
and sooner or later,
everything will work out in your favor.

Maybe you needed that suffering,
even if it was exorbitant
and it was killing you,
to fly to the world of maturity,
where you learn how to deal with obstacles
and you can feel again,
whenever you want,
as a child,
that girl who loved without measure,
who could laugh and cry at the same time.
The roses of your life have finally escaped
of those painful thorns,
that caused you deep wounds.

Even the scarf in which
you are wrapped up all your life,
that each one of us possesses,
has been intensely colored in vivid colors,

getting rid of that sordid gray.
Out of the clouds of smoke,
it came that shining sun,
which embraces you so strongly.
It was born again
only to make you smile easily,
gradually more often.
You squeeze love so tenderly
in your chest again,
you feel it so sweet,
as if it is alive…
Too easily it sometimes falls
between your fingers
and too hard you can win it,
despite the immeasurable efforts made.

What we would have wanted

Sometimes I wonder
what we need to achieve every dream
or what needs to be changed.
Ambition is not enough,
desire is not enough.
I do not know what is needed,
what is the magic ingredient.
I'm disappointed I haven't found it yet.
Me, the person who always gets
what she wants,
no longer exists.
I'm not like that anymore.
I don't know what I want anymore.
My thoughts are scattered,
They are haunting crazy in my head.
I don't know if I like what I have now,
I don't know if I wanted it,
I don't know if I will ever have
what will make me completely happy.
In fact, what makes me happy?
Why do I love the intangible so much?
Why do I want to have
what I cannot have,
because of morale,
because of the lack of impulse,
when its presence is indispensable?

What do I want?
I wish there were no consequences
for a certain period.
I want to do
what I want at that moment,
without thinking about the future,
without thinking about the subsequent regrets.

Damn regrets,
damn feelings,
damn all this life.
I didn't want to be like that.
Why do I sometimes feel
like everyone else knows how to live
and I'm the only one who can barely survive?
Why does everyone think I'm weird,
why am I so weird?
Why doesn't anyone see me?
Why do I have to be so helpless?

I don't know what I want anymore,
I don't even know how I feel anymore…
I would like to start again,
I would like someone to let me know
when I'm going to make a mistake,
to be able to avoid it.
I don't want the life I have anymore.
With few exceptions,
there's nothing good about it.
It's just malice, envy, lack of support…
I would need so much time,
I wish I could do so many things,
but I have so many restraints,
there are so many things that stop me,
there are so many people that discourage me.
Why can't I be strong anymore?
Where did my power go?
Is that all I could bear?
Why can't I do more?
Damn this weakness!
I don't want myself like that anymore,
I don't want to be like that anymore!

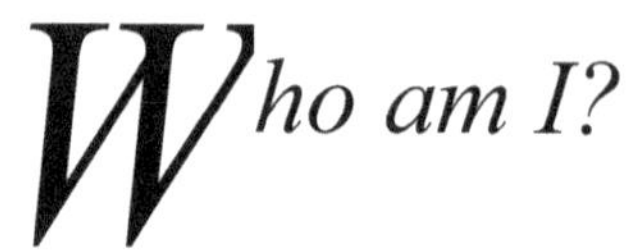 Who am I?

First of all,
I am someone just like everyone else,
a mortal who clings to everything
to live longer.
What really makes us different
is the power to overcome obstacles,
mistakes and disappointments.
Physical appearance is
of the utmost importance.
As far as John Fowles used to say,
"Beauty is something to add.
Like the wrapping around the gift.
It's not the gift itself."
Much more important is
everyone's thinking and soul.
Sometimes I don't accept mine,
I wish I could change them.
Because of this, I often have to lose,
especially being a perfectionist.
Many times, I feel so innocuous, weak,
as if I inspire compassion.
When I need help,
Nobody gives it to me...
I'm so alone!
I also feel disappointed
when I can't do everything,
when I don't live up to the expectations.
I'm almost never happy with myself.
The multitude of aspirations I possess,
I am so afraid that I will not succeed,
that I will not be able to reach
as high as I want.

In conclusion,
in this "tiny" world,
each "me" tries more or less
to integrate and cope with various situations,
to individualize
and show others the strength they have.

Debility

I am alone again
and I begin to tremble from the cold,
from fear…
another day in which I hope and cry,
in which I no longer trust myself.
I would expect a miracle,
but what if I don't believe in them?
Sometimes I really don't understand
my facial expression,
my body language
and the essence of my feelings
or maybe I don't understand the others.
Am I all wrong or
am I the only one doing this?
But I do everything so well,
with so much involvement!
Everyone has left their mark on my soul.
Bizarrely, either by a single glance,
by offering noble feelings
or by contempt, envy and mockery.
I want so much and although I said I could,
now I have no strength.
I need so much protection,
love, respect
or simply the presence of someone
to be with me.
Sometimes I don't understand
why it's so much evil around me,
why everything can't be perfect
and we have to suffer,
even for someone's absence,
for a shed tear,
for someone who doesn't understand
our mentality.

I feel a lot and yet
I can't express it so easy.
I wish I had the opportunity to dream more,
to be able to project my dreams
and to have someone
to share my euphoria with.
I need that whole unit!
Despite all these things,
I will always try to be
with my head up
and face the difficulties,
because I have always been
a strong person
and I do not intend to be
knocked down so easily.
I will try to overcome this weakness,
this evil that constantly grinds me.

*D*ifficulties

Ever since you were in your mother's womb,
you were sad,
disappointed by what you felt,
because you felt her intentions,
you felt that you would become
a little nuisance,
that maybe because of her
you are sometimes so gloomy.
You have no hope,
no more dreams,
even useless ones,
only to remember the moments
when your tears run
through every part of your lips,
not the ones when
you can embrace the euphoria.
Maybe you wish you weren't like that,
you would have liked to receive more love...
On the other hand,
you miss the caresses and hugs
that once relieved your pain.
Somehow, now they are gone too,
they got lost in this sharp fog.
You feel so alone, as usual...
and it's so hard that
you can't share this pain with anyone,
that you have to (or don't?) shut yourself in,
that you cry endlessly,
that you're the same child
crying on sad songs,
who never ceases to feel guilty,
even for the best things,
who may deserve much more,
who trembles in pain.

This child, who is yourself,
needs only protection,
love and respect,
things that can never be found together.
You are so childish
when you look envious at those
who live love stories,
but only in movies...
you are aware that you will continue like this,
that you will be skeptical,
unconscious,
childish,
too loving,
caring
and, above all,
someone who knows
how to love with all her heart...

# Failure

I start by saying that
lately I feel more and more innocuous
and everything seems to be against me.
That enchantment before
was a fictional one,
maybe only in my imagination.
I still don't realize the meaning of all things,
not even the significant ones.
Not even the light
that meets my dark eyes can help me.
This "fall" from heaven was so unexpected,
and you...
you proved to be a demon
that gave me the illusion that
I had caught wings to fly,
when in fact I was buried as deep as possible.
My dream was shattered in an instant
and, without intention,
I found one of the symbols
that confused me in the past.

I wish my maturity had appeared earlier
and I could have mobilized more easily.
Do my feelings come back?
But which of them,
because my heart has lived
in a continuous tumult,
 possessing them all?
I wish I could get into the game
of these contradictory feelings,
to resort to various tricks
and overcome love feelings.
If I had at least one hope
that I could cling to,

a shoulder that I could lean on,
a look in which to observe support,
a HIM...
So small and so disappointed.
I still can't believe that
as much wrong as I was,
I deserve to suffer so much. I feel so alone,
They are gone and I am without anyone here,
In this corner, in this closed world that
I have created it over the days.
You know... maybe you will always stay
In a corner of my heart, but the happiness
I will have in the future
Will compensate with the suffering
You offered me and not even I
Won't know you still exist in that corner
(I've been repeating the same thing for so long...).
I miss my childhood, my family and...
My old self so much!

Hesitation

I am convinced that, at some point,
everyone hesitated
to do, to say, to feel something,
whether it was a forgiveness,
a regret,
a "I love you" or a "I hate you".
But even those hesitations
are benevolent...
Indeed, sometimes we do it for a good reason,
but other times?
Why is it so hard to express your feelings,
to show your insides
and say what you think?
Is it fearful?
Anyway, everything is imminent...
We just cling to insignificant things
and throw away the ones that are of real value.
I admit, maybe I was too hesitant...
maybe if I didn't own them,
my present would have been easier,
I would have smiled more often
and I would have shown everyone
that at any moment, no matter how hard,
I will be able to have whatever I want,
but no...
I'm lying to myself useless!
I don't realize why I divulge so many secrets,
why I'm so transparent sometimes
and why I don't accept my failures...
I don't live in that bright paradise anymore,
because, unconsciously,
I matured much too early.
I preferred to endure those moments
when I was immature,

when I took suffering as happiness
and always had my eyes closed,
living in constant bliss.
Even now, I hesitate to believe
that I can't go back in time,
that I can't relive certain moments
and that I have to face this cruel reality,
a reality that I cannot accept,
because of the superficiality of everyone.
I hope it's because of fatigue
and I'll wake up in the morning.

*T*houghts

You are waiting for everything to change,
for you to leave or
for everyone else to leave.
You are still not sure
that you made the right choice,
but not the wrong one.
You just have to be patient,
observe the evolution of things
and only then draw various conclusions.
Have you always been like this?
You fought for what you wanted,
just so then, when you fulfilled your dream,
you gave up?
How distrustful you are!
On top of that,
you should see the problems
from another perspective.
Try to feel every heartbeat,
every dream that can be projected
into the future,
every ecstatic moment!
You may not have another chance,
you may lose far too much
because of your little childish whims.
How have you grown up,
if you still "love" to suffer?
What about the efforts made?
The support received and the false promises?
I tend to think that
you are not trying to do anything
to avoid these tumultuous blows.
On the contrary...
You take advantage of this combination of
grace and the "tragedy" of your life.

Can't you just use grace?
Do you think you can't have the strength
to continue without suffering?
Do you think it's all that difficult every time?
You should destroy your skepticism,
stop for at least a second
and look at everything in the shadows.
It is very likely that everything
will turn pink
and you will be envious of yourself,
even as perfectionist as you are.
Although not everything is like a pattern,
you will realize that you have
the most beautiful things,
things that few have.
Didn't you say that a new day has come
and that today you will fight,
more than ever,
for what you truly desire?
Where this affirmation stands?
Do you deny that it was once yours
or do you intend to keep
your point of view?
You know...
you should appreciate what you have,
before it's too late,
before you are left with only memories.
Appreciate and love,
in spite of everything
that has happened to you!
Otherwise, you will not warm yourself
in the arms of happiness!

*T*ears

I just needed support, that's all.
That way I could have fully enjoyed
the success, the ecstatic moments.
But since everything couldn't be perfect,
it was absolutely necessary
for you to show up and destroy me,
to destroy my hopes,
to make me stop believing in my talents,
in my power to go on,
to face chance as I did
when you were not with me.
In these moments, I don't love you anymore.
I want you away.
I want you to leave and leave me alone. However,
you could be more subtle.
I think I can strongly say
that all the other things I receive are worthless.

Yes I'm ambitious,
but that doesn't mean
I can be strong indefinitely
and, no matter what happens,
I can follow my dreams.
I can't go on,
I can't fight anymore.
I will give up this too because of you.
Your exorbitant love hurts me… deeply!
I refuse to receive it again.
Gradually that period comes,
 when I just want to hide,
to get away from this evil that worries me.
I want to get lost somwhere
you can't find me anymore.

My ambiguous thoughts
don't seem to give me peace of mind.
Neither do they?
I want everything to end!
I don't know if I can stand it anymore,
because I'm starting to get skeptical,
I don't believe in myself.
Only if f I could control everything,
if a miracle happened
and I changed my character...
I'm still demoralized.
But, for sure,
I will remain the same young woman
who suffers even for nothing,
who pours her bitterness into writing.

I miss

I miss love,
I miss ingenuity and childishness,
the moments when I loved with passion,
even though those who received my love
did not deserve it.
I wish I could look into the past
without a tear coming.
I miss my childhood
and the moments when I wasn't so affected
by someone's inattention,
by someone's indifference,
by the annoying comments of my parents
and by those sarcastic jokes
of my high school classmates.
I miss making compromises,
not hiding what I feel,
to have the imprint of someone in my soul
and to feel protected,
even if this would be as it was in a certain past.
I just want to feel the love in my arms,
to warm up with it,
to cool off with it,
to feel her penetrating every pore of mine.
The current one is unreal,
sordid,
pharisaical.
It's not love anymore,
it's habit,
attachment.
After all, it had never been love.
I was just trying to make it look like this,
to spend a few more seconds without suffering,
to try to get drunk in bliss.
I miss so many things

that I don't know which one to start with.
The ones that really made me happy
or the ones that hurt me,
even though I adored them,
deified them,
embraced them more deeply than the others?
What a candid child!
I shouldn't even miss it,
I shouldn't love it anymore.
I should just fly and be a simple traveler!

Moments

There are times when you want to go back,
to be able to make compromises,
to be able to fight for
The bliss in which you live
cannot be stolen from you,
it is yours until the moment you give it up,
consciously or not.
Maybe your thoughts (or, rather, sentiments)
are ambiguous,
maybe your bitter lips
need a gram of honey.
Everything seems to have changed:
the banal has become complex,
the love has been transformed
into an impure and simple feeling,
the hatred has risen on the scale of intensity
to the highest level.

The looks of others are so ambiguous,
their expressionless faces,
their bodies devoid of any admiration.
They may have something beautiful,
but they have known the art of concealment.
Besides, your hesitations
do not seem to have an end.
They continue unknowingly.
Power... the power to move on,
to be indifferent,
to fight only for one's own interests...
in what desert has it now disappeared?

The horizon seems gloomy,
the clouds (non-existent) seem to
bring storms (in your heart).

Again the pessimism!
It will never disappear.
Again pessimism,
but the sun seems to smile.
Just close your eyes!

There are times when you just want to stop,
do nothing, just shut up.
Shut up!
You just want to look,
feel,
think
and love again!
Yes... that feeling that leads you to ecstasy
Has disappeared for some time.
The heart also feels empty at times
And the thoughts can only look
In the direction of insignificant things,
Because the others have disappeared.
You often want to drain
Like sand on the glass of a broken hourglass,
Then drown in the azure waves of the sea.
There are times when you just want to
Breathe easy and look the beautiful,
Without implying anything else.

Protagonist

Leave me alone!
That's all I want to tell you…
you don't even do anything,
you just exist and your presence hurts me,
it used to.
I don't even know anymore.
I thought I forgot,
I thought I didn't miss us.
In fact...
now I don't know if it's missing at all!
I hate you, you know?
I wish so much
that you would no longer be
the protagonist of my creations.
I wish you could just exist for her...

You know... it hurts a lot,
even if I don't talk about love now,
I don't write anything about it anymore.
Now I just feel angry.
How could I be so naive?
Why did I let so much time pass,
time I cried for you,
in which I suffered unnecessarily?
Did this suffering lead me to something good?
To look at the good side of things?
But what is it?
Damn! I can't find any.
Except that you always have been my muse.
I can't find another benefit.
I wish you wouldn't inspire me anymore,
to free me from these stupid nets.
I hate the blue of your eyes,
your breath,

your lips,
your face,
everything... you know?

Leave me alone!
How grateful I would be
if I only remembered you as a simple man.
How could you have the strength
to enter into my heart so easily
and not intend to go out?
What did I do wrong
for you to punish myself
in this atrocious way?

And yet you do nothing to me,
but you have done enough for me in the past.
You have taken advantage of me,
of my ingenuity!
You should have warned me, demon!
You're a demon!
I don't know another word
that would better characterize you
and be pleasing to your ear.
Why being pleasing to your ear?
I hate myself because of you!
I no longer have ambition,
I no longer have confidence,
I no longer have love to offer...
you took everything from me, demon!
How I wish I could tell you,
from the bottom of my heart,
that I hate you!
However, I will do it,
even if the following words
were never plausible: I hate you!

Regrets

I'm sorry…
I think these are the right words!
I wish I could appreciate the right things,
the ones that really value.
I wish I could nurture the feelings I want,
I would like to stop having this heart,
to replace it
and to be able to command it,
to be able to overcome
the barriers of the probable.
Why can't I go back to heaven or...
have I ever been there?
I tend to think so,
because you made me feel
important and special,
you loved me,
you protected me
and it mattered a lot to me,
but not as it should have been...
Why are certain moments so ephemeral?
Why don't I feel the heat anymore?
Honestly, I miss you...
but don't ask me why,
because I don't know what to say to you!
I prefer the present,
although it is painful,
although I cry
and maybe tomorrow I would smile.
Despite the fact
that I feel again strong wounds,
now I will not move away,
I stay here with you,
maybe you will need me.
Why is life so unfair sometimes?

Why isn't our relationship with it fair?
I've felt its revenge so many times
and I can't understand why.
Was I so wrong?
I don't want to suffer anymore,
to cry,
to live in the dark
and to see only a few remnants of love.
Maybe there would have been more, right?
Certainly you would have offered me
that whole unit.
Why didn't I accept it?
And... I don't know how, but... I love you!

It would seem

It would seem that everything is perfect,
that there are a multitude
of noble feelings between us
and that this relationship is based on respect.
But why lie to ourselves,
why hide everything,
why not support our opinions?
Just to please others,
to be mocked by them in an atrocious way?
No! An infinite number of times no!
Honestly, I'm tired of this lie called life,
of the envy and wickedness
that lingers between us,
of this constant pessimism.
I really want to have love,
sincerity,
kindness,
but it's so hard for me to get it.

It would seem that nothing is easy,
that you have to fight for everything.
But then why is it so easy to hate,
to be bad and instead
so difficult to say *I love you, I was wrong*
or to do something simple,
but something that matters a lot to someone?
I don't understand anything,
I don't understand this life!

It would seem that I am optimistic,
that I am trapped
in this mirage of maturity
and that I accept it.
What a lie!

To be honest, I am optimistic,
but when it makes no sense
and this state disappears quickly,
because, at every moment,
someone is responsible to blame me,
to ruin my happiness,
to say exactly what I do not want to hear.
In conclusion , the pessimism still dominates.
Do you see?
Otherwise, I wouldn't tell you these things,
probably dull,
I would delight you with a lively dance,
energetic of words...
Aw, how much I would change!
How much I would do for another soul,
a more impassive one,
for another mentality,
a more optimistic one,
for another ME,
a totally distinct one.

It would seem I'm unhappy,
but I'm not.
It's too hard for someone to be satisfied
with so little.
You tell me!
I'm not realistic?
This is how I see myself.
Why should I say some false words?
Why shouldn't I tell the truth?
This is how I perceive it as I said before!
Thus, I will let you remain forever
in a non-existent,
intangible fuzz,
in a sordid fuzz!

*F*eeling

I want to discover your riddles,
to force you to make me love you,
not to stop you belonging to me,
even though you are not mine yet.
I just hope that the moment
when you will be ready to face the chance,
to discover your feelings enough,
to arrive soon.
Maybe there are moments
when I would like to reveal my feelings to you,
to thank you, in my own way,
for being by my side,
even when I'm trying to get away.
Yes, that would be an option,
but aren't I ambitious?
Didn't I learn from you to be optimistic?
And I will fight for what I want,
for you,
more than ever!
I promise you!
In fact, I should only say how I feel.
I don't know why I judge you
for something I am not able to achieve either.
Honestly, often I just want
you to hold me in your arms,
nothing more.
I think that would be enough to start our story.
How beautiful it sounds!
Something of ours...
Will it ever be?
Won't it be too late,
when we have the courage we need?
I wouldn't want to be sad. Help me again!